THE TALE OF
PETER RABBIT

BY BEATRIX POTTER

FREDERICK WARNE

ONCE upon a time there were four little Rabbits, and their names were—Flopsy, Mopsy, Cotton-tail, and Peter.

They lived with their Mother in a sand-bank, underneath the root of a very big fir-tree.

Hello Dear Friends,

This wonderful book and all of the books to follow are a special gift for you. If one wish of mine could come true, I hope my Imagination Library gives wings to all of your dreams.

The Tale of Peter Rabbit, as your first book of this wonderful programme, seems to be just the right place for me to share these words with you:

> *Try to be the first one up the mountain,*
> *The highest flying dreamer in the sky.*
> *Try your best to be an inspiration*
> *For others that are still afraid and shy.*
> *Try to make the most of every moment*
> *If you fail, get up and try again.*
> *Try each day a little harder*
> *If you never try, you never win.*

I hope you love these books and enjoy the precious memories they will create.

Love,

Dolly

FREDERICK WARNE

UK | USA | Canada | Ireland | Australia
India | New Zealand | South Africa

Frederick Warne is part of the Penguin Random House group of companies
whose addresses can be found at global.penguinrandomhouse.com.

www.penguin.co.uk   www.puffin.co.uk   www.ladybird.co.uk

First published 1902 by Frederick Warne
This edition with new reproduction of Beatrix Potter's book illustrations published 2006

014

Printed in Italy

The authorized representative in the EEA is Penguin Random House Ireland,
Morrison Chambers, 32 Nasstau Street, Dublin D02 YH68

A CIP catalogue record for this book is available from the British Library

ISBN: 978–0–723–26332–6

All correspondence to:
Frederick Warne, Penguin Random House Children's
One Embassy Gardens, 8 Viaduct Gardens, London SW11 7BW

"NOW, my dears," said old Mrs. Rabbit one
morning, "you may go into the fields or down the
lane, but don't go into Mr. McGregor's garden.
Your Father had an accident there; he was put in
a pie by Mrs. McGregor."

"NOW run along, and don't get into mischief. I am going out."
Then old Mrs. Rabbit took a basket and her umbrella, and went through the wood to the baker's. She bought a loaf of brown bread and five currant buns.

FLOPSY, Mopsy, and Cotton-tail, who were good little bunnies, went down the lane to gather blackberries;

BUT Peter, who was very naughty, ran straight away to Mr. McGregor's garden, and squeezed under the gate!

FIRST he ate some lettuces and some French beans; and then he ate some radishes;

AND then, feeling rather sick, he went to look for some parsley.

BUT round the end of a cucumber frame, whom should he meet but Mr. McGregor!

Mr. McGregor was on his hands and knees planting out young cabbages, but he jumped up and ran after Peter, waving a rake and calling out, "Stop thief!"

PETER was most dreadfully frightened; he rushed all over the garden, for he had forgotten the way back to the gate.

He lost one of his shoes among the cabbages, and the other shoe amongst the potatoes.

AFTER losing them, he ran on four legs and went faster, so that I think he might have got away altogether if he had not unfortunately run into a gooseberry net, and got caught by the large buttons on his jacket. It was a blue jacket with brass buttons, quite new.

PETER gave himself up for lost, and shed big
tears; but his sobs were overheard by some friendly
sparrows, who flew to him in great excitement, and
implored him to exert himself.

MR. McGREGOR came up with a sieve, which he intended to pop upon the top of Peter; but Peter wriggled out just in time, leaving his jacket behind him.

AND rushed into the
tool-shed, and jumped
into a can. It would
have been a
beautiful thing to
hide in, if it had not
had so much water
in it.

Mr. McGregor was
quite sure that Peter
was somewhere in the
tool-shed, perhaps hidden underneath a
flower-pot. He began to turn them over carefully,
looking under each.

Presently Peter sneezed—"Kertyschoo!"
Mr. McGregor was after him in no time,

AND tried to put his foot upon Peter, who jumped out of a window, upsetting three plants. The window was too small for Mr. McGregor, and he was tired of running after Peter. He went back to his work.

PETER sat down to rest; he was out of breath
and trembling with fright, and he had not the least
idea which way to go. Also he was very damp with
sitting in that can.

  After a time
he began to
wander about,
going lippity—
lippity—not
very fast, and
looking all
round.

HE found a door in a wall; but it was locked, and there was no room for a fat little rabbit to squeeze underneath.

An old mouse was running in and out over the stone door-step, carrying peas and beans to her family in the wood. Peter asked her the way to the gate, but she had such a large pea in her mouth that she could not answer. She only shook her head at him. Peter began to cry.

THEN he tried to find his way straight across the garden, but he became more and more puzzled. Presently, he came to a pond where Mr. McGregor filled his water-cans. A white cat was staring at some

gold-fish; she sat very, very still, but now and then the tip of her tail twitched as if it were alive. Peter thought it best to go away without speaking to her; he had heard about cats from his cousin, little Benjamin Bunny.

HE went back towards the tool-shed, but
suddenly, quite close to him, he heard the noise
of a hoe—scr-r-ritch, scratch, scratch, scritch. Peter
scuttered underneath the bushes. But presently, as
nothing happened, he came out, and climbed upon
a wheelbarrow and peeped over. The first thing he
saw was Mr. McGregor hoeing onions. His back
was turned towards Peter, and beyond him was

the gate!
 Peter got down
very quietly off the
wheelbarrow, and
started running as fast
as he could go, along
a straight walk behind
some black-currant
bushes.

MR. McGREGOR caught sight of him at
the corner, but Peter did not care. He slipped
underneath the gate, and was safe at last in the
wood outside the garden.

MR. McGREGOR hung up the little jacket
and the shoes for a scarecrow to frighten the
blackbirds.

PETER never stopped running or looked behind
him till he got home to the big fir-tree.

He was so tired that he flopped down upon
the nice soft sand on the floor of the rabbit-hole
and shut his eyes. His mother was busy cooking;
she wondered what
he had done with
his clothes. It
was the second
little jacket
and pair of
shoes that
Peter had
lost in a
fortnight!

I AM sorry to say that Peter was not very well
during the evening.

His mother put him to bed, and made some
camomile tea; and she gave a dose of it to Peter!

"One table-spoonful to be taken at bed-time."

BUT Flopsy, Mopsy, and Cotton-tail had bread and milk and blackberries for supper.